JOURNEY BEYOND
THE VILLAGE
WALL AND INTO
DANGER.

◊▽◊▽◊▽◊▽◊▽◊▽◊

DISCOVER A NEW WORLD OF
INCREDIBLE MONSTERS.

◊▽◊▽◊▽◊▽◊▽◊▽◊

CAN LEO KEEP THE SECRET OF
THE GUARDIANS?

◊▽◊▽◊▽◊▽◊▽◊▽◊

WHERE WILL LEO'S MAP
TAKE HIM NEXT?

First American Edition 2022
Kane Miller, A Division of EDC Publishing

Text copyright © Kris Humphrey 2020
Illustrations copyright © Pete Williamson 2020
Leo's Map of Monsters: The Armored Goretusk was originally
published in English in 2020. This edition is published by
arrangement with Oxford University Press.

For information contact:
Kane Miller, A Division of EDC Publishing
5402 S 122nd E Ave
Tulsa, OK 74146
www.kanemiller.com
www.myubam.com

Library of Congress Control Number: 2021948326

Printed and bound in the United States of America
1 2022

ISBN: 978-1-68464-485-8

LEO'S MAP OF MONSTERS

MONSTERS

THE ARMORED GORETUSK

KRIS HUMPHREY

ILLUSTRATED BY

PETE WILLIAMSON

Kane Miller
A DIVISION OF EDC PUBLISHING

NORTHERN
MOUNTAINS

CLAY
DESERT

THE EASTERN
RIVERS

EASTERN
PLAINS

ONE

Everyone knows you don't go out into the forest. That's why the village elders built the Wall—years and years ago, longer than anyone can remember. They built it to keep us safe from all the deadly forest creatures: the ruthless wolf packs, the huge ravenous bears, and the wildcats with their razor-sharp claws.

It's why they built the watchtowers and the gates, why the rules are so strict about who can leave the village and how far they can go.

The forest is wild and dark and full of nothing but danger.

At least that's what everyone thinks.

And that's what I thought too, until the morning of my ninth birthday.

◂ ◊ Δ ◊ ▸

Some kids are terrified of their ninth birthday, and you can't really blame them for that. You wake up and there's a letter waiting

2

for you, telling you what Assignment you'll be doing for the next two years.

All you get is a word or two: goat tender, muck shoveler, woodchopper—whatever the elders decide. And that's the next two years mapped out for you, just like that.

But me? I wasn't scared at all.

I was pretty sure the elders would assign me to the Records Office where my best friend, Jacob, already worked. They tried to match your Assignment to your talents, and I was good at reading and writing. I was also really good at staying indoors. It was going to be great.

So when I woke up on my birthday, I climbed out of bed feeling pretty excited.

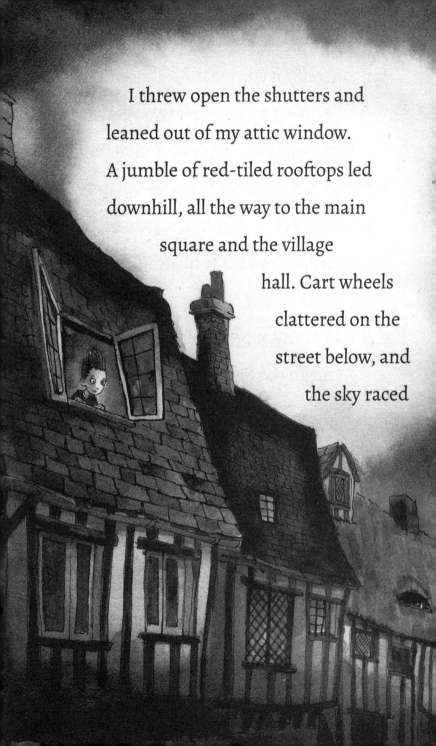

I threw open the shutters and leaned out of my attic window. A jumble of red-tiled rooftops led downhill, all the way to the main square and the village hall. Cart wheels clattered on the street below, and the sky raced with wispy clouds. I peered back up the street toward Jacob's house, but his window was closed. Jacob never gets out of bed before he absolutely has to.

I hurried down the ladder onto the first-floor landing, then down the stairs to the living room. Mum was kneeling beside the stove, feeding it with logs. When she heard me, she turned and rushed over.

"Leo!" she said, grabbing me into a powerful hug. "Happy birthday, son."

She kissed my forehead, and I wiped it off immediately.

"Thanks," I said.

Behind her, on a high shelf, I couldn't help noticing a small package decorated with sprigs of ivy: my birthday present. It was a set of charcoal drawing pencils, and I knew this because Lulu, my older sister, had never kept a secret in her life.

The back door thumped, and in walked Lulu, carrying her basket of woodworking tools, closely followed by Stickle the cat.

Lulu grinned at me. "It's here," she said, dropping her basket with a clank. "Are you going to open it now?"

For a second I wasn't sure what she was talking about; then my eyes settled on the table. It was set with jam and butter, and there was a jug of flowers in the center. Propped against the flower jug was a small rectangle of paper.

The letter.

For the first time, I felt a shiver of nerves. What had the elders chosen for me?

"Oh, come on," said Lulu. "We all know you're going to the Records Office. You virtually live there anyway!" She grabbed my arm and dragged me over to the table. "Open it, Leo. Put us out of our misery."

"Open it when you're ready," Mum said. "It's your big day, my love. No one else's."

I sat down, lifting the letter carefully. My name was written on the front: *Leo Wilder*, in thin, slanted letters. It was sealed on the reverse side with a circle of bloodred wax.

"Here," Mum said, placing a bread roll and a cup of goat's milk in front of me.

"Thanks," I said, but I didn't feel like eating.

I touched the wax seal on the letter and noticed Lulu glaring at me impatiently from across the table.

"Fine," I said, sliding my finger under one of the folds. The wax cracked, and the letter opened just a little.

I paused, took a deep breath, then pulled the letter open and read the words that were written there—the command of the elders, my Assignment for the next two years.

"Huh?"

I dropped the letter and stood up, knocking the table so that everything shook. My cup teetered and fell, sloshing goat's milk onto my feet.

"What is it?" Lulu asked. "Where are you going?"

I felt Stickle at my feet, lapping up the spilled milk. Then Mum was suddenly beside me, gently squeezing my shoulder.

"Oh my," she said. "Well, I've never seen *that* before."

The letter lay open on the tabletop, two words inked in black:

TOP SECRET.

Lulu hurried round the table to read the letter.

"What does it mean?" she said.

But there was no answer, because none of us knew.

Then, there came a knock at the door.

For an instant, I thought Jacob had arrived.

How could I tell him I wasn't coming to the Records Office, that we wouldn't be spending our Assignments together after all?

But, I realized, it couldn't possibly be Jacob. He never knocked, he just walked right in.

So who was it?

Mum glanced down at me, the same question furrowing her brow. She gave my shoulder a final squeeze before cautiously moving toward the door.

The hinges creaked and light poured in from the street. I saw a tall, slim outline on the doorstep and heard a surprised tone in my mother's voice.

"Oh . . . good morning . . . please, uh . . . please come in."

Ducking gracefully under the door frame came Gilda, the Village Chief.

She glanced at me as she entered, her long green cloak brushing the floor. Then she turned and smiled at Mum.

"Good morning," she said. "I'm so sorry for the intrusion."

"Not at all," Mum replied. She glanced at the spillage on the table, and her cheeks flushed in embarrassment. "Can I get you anything? Uh . . . Would you like some milk?"

"Thank you, no," replied the chief with a polite smile.

Then her smile vanished, and she looked me straight in the eye. "But I'm afraid I do have to borrow your son."

TWo

Gilda led me through the bustling morning streets. She'd removed her distinctive green cloak and pulled up the hood of an old gray coat she'd been wearing underneath.

"We mustn't be seen," she said. "So keep quiet, all right?"

I didn't like being ordered about like this—especially on my birthday—but

15

I knew better than to argue with the Village Chief.

Eventually, we arrived at a quiet cobbled street that ran alongside the towering Village Wall. Gilda stopped outside a low wooden building. She glanced around and then shoved the door open.

Inside, an old man slouched on a tiny

stool, fast asleep and snoring. All around him lay baskets filled with turnips.

"No way," I said. "I am *not* working for the turnip man."

"Keep your voice down," Gilda whispered, leading me through into a second room.

"Your Assignment isn't in the village," she said, moving to the back wall and pushing her hand into a tiny crevice in the wood. She made a twisting motion and something clunked. The next thing I knew, the wall was swinging outward, and a breeze was flowing in, carrying the smell of damp earth and the whisper of rustling leaves.

"Come on," said Gilda.

"But that's . . ."

"Yes," she said, smiling. "The forest."

◄ ◇ △ ◇ ◄

All around us the trees swayed like giants. I glanced about nervously, expecting to be attacked at any moment by a wildcat or a boar or a hungry pack of wolves. Before this, the closest I'd ever been to the forest was looking at the treetops from my bedroom window.

Now here I was, walking through that hidden world.

There was a crashing sound nearby, and we both stopped dead. Gilda stared into the trees.

"What is it?" I asked.

"Probably just a squirrel," Gilda murmured unconvincingly.

I glanced behind me and realized that I could no longer see the Wall.

"I think we've come too far," I whispered.

"It's all right," Gilda said, continuing along the path. "Just try to keep up."

"But what about the village rules?" I asked. "Even the woodcutters have to stay in sight of the Wall. There could be bears, or thieves, or . . ."

Gilda stopped and turned, giving me an impatient look.

"Leo," she said. "I'm aware of the village rules. And yes, the forest can be a dangerous place. But some tasks require us to break those rules. Now please, will you just follow me?"

A few minutes later, we came to a smooth pointed rock that stood about as high as my chest. Here, we left the path and pushed our way through a thicket of thorny shrubs. I had to concentrate hard on avoiding the thorns, so I didn't see the cabin until it was looming over me.

Its walls were strung with cobwebs and its roof covered with moss. The door was narrow and crooked, and its one small window was tightly shuttered. It looked abandoned, as if the forest was trying to swallow it up.

"Well," said Gilda. "I hope he's in."

"Someone *lives* here?" I asked.

But Gilda ignored me, already knocking at the door.

Uneven footsteps thumped inside. Then the door creaked open. I saw the stooping outline of a man silhouetted against flickering candlelight.

"Henrik." Gilda greeted him with a nod.

The man let out a grunt.

"Took your sweet time," he muttered, hobbling back inside.

"In you go," Gilda said to me.

"Do I have to?" I asked.

"Yes," she said. "You do."

The room was large and cluttered with a mind-boggling array of objects. There were books, scrolls, and ironbound chests, skulls with and without horns, items so strange I had no idea if they were exotic ornaments or deadly weapons.

The man, Henrik, sat behind a battered old writing desk. He was tall and thin. His hair was drawn back into a ponytail, mostly gray, but with streaks of the bright red it must once have been.

"So this is him?" Henrik said, eyeing me suspiciously. "Bit scrawny isn't he? You sure he's the right one?"

Gilda nodded. "He's the one."

"He'd better be," said Henrik. "We don't have much time."

He gave me another unimpressed look, as if he'd been handed a rotten apple for his lunch.

"Much time for what?" I asked Gilda. "What am I doing here?"

She shushed me with a stern glance, then moved closer to the old man, both of them acting as if I wasn't there.

"Everything's ready?" Gilda asked him in a low, urgent voice.

"Of course," Henrik muttered. "Well, one slight hitch, but . . . it's ready."

Gilda frowned. "You don't seem very sure," she replied.

"I told you it would be ready, and it's ready," Henrik growled. "It's up to the boy now."

"Well, in that case . . ." Gilda began.

"Excuse me!" I interrupted. "Is anyone going to tell me what's going on?"

They both stared at me.

"You haven't told him?" the old man grumbled at Gilda.

"Well . . ." Gilda began.

But Henrik cut her off, fixing me with an intense stare.

"You'll have heard a lot of talk about bears and wildcats and wolves," he said to me. "About how dangerous the forest is. Am I right, lad?"

I nodded.

"Well, what if I told you there are no

bears? No wildcats or wolves either. Not in *this* forest."

He watched me closely. But I didn't know what to say to that. It didn't make any sense.

"But . . . the Wall?" I stuttered finally. "That's what it's for, isn't it? Keeping the wild animals out?"

"Wild things, yes," the old man replied. "But not the kind you're thinking of."

"Then what?" I asked, not sure I wanted to hear the answer.

Henrik grinned, a sly, foreboding grin.

"Monsters, boy. The Wall's there to keep you safe from monsters."

I felt a strange shiver down my spine.

Obviously, this man was crazy. But when I glanced at Gilda, she just nodded back at me solemnly.

"You heard me right, lad," Henrik said.

He kept me fixed with his stare, as if he was trying to frighten me.

"What kind of . . . monsters?" I asked.

"More kinds than you can imagine," he replied. "They've been roaming this forest since the dawn of time. The mountains, too, and the lands beyond."

"Are they dangerous?" I asked.

"Dangerous?" Henrik limped across the room and grabbed a sharpened piece of bone about as long as my leg. "You see this? It came from a Lake-Lurker's mouth.

They have fifty-five of these—*in each jaw*. Is that dangerous enough for you, boy?"

I figured it was a rhetorical question, but I nodded anyway.

"Well," said Gilda, awkwardly. "They don't all have teeth like that. Just some of them."

"Yes, yes," Henrik said. "Mostly they're fine. But some of them . . . Well, that's what I'm here for. It's what *you're* here for now."

I felt a cold rush of fear. "Me?" I said.

Gilda nodded. "Henrik is our Guardian," she said. "He protects the village from monsters. This is your Assignment, Leo. You're going to be a Guardian, too."

I stared in disbelief as Gilda moved toward the door.

"You'll explain what needs to be done?" she asked Henrik.

"I will," the Guardian said, nodding gravely.

"Good luck then, Leo," she said, with

a smile that was probably meant to be reassuring. Then she was gone.

I felt stunned, watching blankly as Henrik limped across the room and began unfolding a large rectangle of paper on top of his desk.

"Come here, lad."

As I drew closer, I saw that there were small dots of light moving across the Guardian's face. The further he unfolded the paper, the more lights appeared, and I realized that they were coming from the paper itself.

All across its waxy surface, dots of different colors moved, some large and slow, some tiny and quick. They moved across a detailed chart of rivers, trees, and mountains, all shown from above—and in the center, surrounded by the Wall, lay the village.

I looked up at Henrik and found him watching me closely.

"This," he said, "is the Map of Monsters."

I peered down at the map, mesmerized by the colored lights.

"Each of these lights is a different monster," he explained. "You see these here?"

He pointed to a group of silver-gray dots clustered in a mountain pass.

"These are Rocksloths," he said. "Maybe a couple of other types in there too. Anyway, all the gray ones are rock monsters. They live in and around the mountains. The size of the light shows what type of rock monster it is. You see?"

I bent over the map and saw that most of the gray dots were the same size, but there were some slightly larger ones as well.

"The color shows the habitat," the Guardian went on. "Green for forest monsters, purple for marsh monsters, blue for river, and gray for rock. There are some other habitats, too, but you won't see them round here."

"What about this one?" I asked, pointing at a large purple light much closer to the village than any of the others.

Henrik smiled at me.

"I was wondering if you'd notice that."

He stepped back from the table and lifted his trouser leg.

"See this?"

His entire lower leg was bandaged, with blotches of red seeping through.

"I've got that monster to thank for it," he said, prodding the purple dot on the map. "That monster," he went on, "is an Armored Goretusk. I found it roaming around near the river, separated from its herd in the Festian Swamps. I tried to turn it back upriver, but the thing got spooked. It charged me. Nearly took my leg off. It's been stomping around the forest all night—and getting closer to the village every minute."

"What are you going to do?" I asked, unable to take my eyes from the foot-long wound on the Guardian's leg.

"I can't go after it," he said. "Too slow. But you look pretty quick, eh, lad?"

"What do you mean?" I didn't much like the mischievous glint in his eyes.

"You're going to turn this monster around."

"But I don't know how to do that!"

"Don't worry," Henrik said. "Here . . ."

He grabbed a small pouch from behind the desk and dropped it onto the map with a dull clank.

"Take a look," he said.

I opened the pouch and saw a collection of small, smooth stones. Henrik placed a battered old slingshot beside it: a y-shaped handle of dark wood, with long, stretchy cords attaching it to the leather sling.

"What am I supposed to do with these?"

"Use the instructions." He reached past me and pulled out a strip of fabric that was sewn into the inside of the pouch. It was embroidered with words and symbols. "You can read, can't you? Gilda

promised she'd bring one who could read."

"Yes, I can read, but this doesn't make any sense. What are all these symbols?"

The Guardian stalked across the room shaking his head. He grabbed a small knapsack from the corner and handed it to me. Inside was a water flask and some bread wrapped in a cloth.

"Listen, boy, we don't have time for all this chatter. That monster could go crashing into the village any minute. It'll probably trample a few villagers, but then the villagers will kill it. And you know what happens after that?"

I shrugged.

"I'll tell you what," he said. "There'll be panic. The secret we Guardians have been keeping for generations will be out—all of that work and sacrifice for nothing. First the villagers will be scared, but then they'll take matters into their own hands. They'll hunt these creatures into extinction."

He gazed down at the constellation of lights on the map, a fierce look in his eyes.

"We're not just here to protect the villagers," he said. "We're protecting the monsters too."

He folded up the map and thrust it at me. "Here," he said. "Time to do your job."

THRee

I knew there was a bright summer sky above the trees, but I couldn't see it.

The ancient oaks of the forest grew close together, tangling their branches to block out the sun. The air was clammy, and full of insects that buzzed around my head and tried as hard as they could to fly up my nose.

I was climbing a steep ridge,

dragging myself over mossy boulders and roots. My legs ached, and my socks still squelched with the milk I'd spilled on them at breakfast. But worst of all was the churning fear in my stomach. I still couldn't quite believe what was happening. Here I was, trekking through the shadowy depths of the forest, expected to save the village from a rampaging monster.

It seemed like a lot of responsibility, and I wondered why Gilda had selected *me* for this task.

With a pang of envy, I pictured Jacob
beginning another quiet morning
in the Records Office. I wondered
what he'd say if I told him the forest
was full of monsters. But that was a
conversation we could never have.

The pouch of stones I'd been given
swung at my belt, with the slingshot
tucked in beside it. Inside were the so-
called instructions, which I
hadn't had the chance
to look at, let alone
decipher. This,
I thought
angrily, was
the only

protection I had. All Henrik had said was that I should *choose my stones wisely*, which was easily the most useless advice I'd ever been given.

The hill seemed to go on forever, so I decided to stop for a rest. I slipped the Map of Monsters from my pocket, and the heavy waxed paper unfolded neatly, revealing the glowing purple dot that marked the location of the monster.

I turned the map around, then turned it back. Uphill still seemed like the right direction. If you could call chasing after a deadly monster "the right direction." Besides the wound it had left in the Guardian's leg, I didn't know much about this Armored Goretusk. But on that evidence alone, I wasn't particularly looking forward to meeting it.

A few minutes later, I reached the summit and began following a thin path that led along the ridge. I clutched the map in my hand and peered nervously into the surrounding trees. Every time a bird or a squirrel rustled in the undergrowth my heart missed a beat. But I kept going, deeper and deeper into the forest.

The path began to curve, and I considered checking the map again, but as I arrived at the edge of a clearing, I realized that I wouldn't have to.

There, in the center of the clearing, was the monster.

I have to say, it wasn't quite the monster I was expecting. In fact, if it was up to me, I'm not sure I'd have called it a monster at all.

It looked like a large, sand-colored weasel—or maybe a small, sand-colored cat—and it was just as furry as either of them. But it also had a pair of black, leathery wings, and it was using them to hover just above the trees on the far side of the clearing. Whatever it was, it had its back to me, its thin, forked tail flicking from side to side.

I stood there wondering what I was supposed to do now. However small this creature looked, it had defeated Henrik and left him with a serious leg wound. I figured it was time to get the slingshot out.

Opening the pouch, I drew out a handful of stones. They all looked the same, but after a quick look at the instructions I knew I had no chance of deciphering them in time. I picked a stone at random and dropped the rest back in.

When I looked up, I saw that the monster was now perched on a high branch at the far end of the clearing. Its amber-colored eyes glared right at me, and I didn't much like the look in them. So, even though it was small and actually kind of cute, I felt that I should load my stone and send a warning shot to scare the creature off.

The trouble was, I'd never used a slingshot before.

As soon as I started fumbling the stone into the sling, the weasel-monster leaped into the air. By the time I'd fitted the stone and drawn back the sling, the monster was halfway across the clearing and swooping down toward me with a mean look on its face.

"STOP!" someone shouted, in an echoey, high-pitched voice that seemed to come from every direction at once.

"STOP! STOP! STOP!"

I twisted round, startled, and
accidentally let go of the sling, sending
the stone directly upward. For a long,
confusing moment I watched the stone
rise into the air and then begin to fall.

Suddenly something furry hit my face,
and I realized the monster was on me.

"AWAY! AWAY! NOW!" the strange
voice echoed.

And at the same time, the monster was
forcing me back into the trees, its paws

gripping tight to my hair and ears, its wings propelling us both from the clearing.

I stumbled back, clutching helplessly at its wriggling body, as my nose and mouth were smothered in its belly fur.

I tried to shout for help, but the creature only flapped its wings harder, sending us crashing into the undergrowth.

I lost my balance completely, and as I hit the forest floor, a deafening BOOM shook the air and a wave of hot air swept over me. The beast was suddenly gone from my face, and I saw a thin pillar of blue-green flame rising above the trees.

Nearby, the undergrowth was burning, and I jumped to my feet, coughing as the smoke hit my lungs. I stumbled away from the fire, finding my way back into the clearing. The spot where I'd been standing was now a charred circle of burnt grass, and the tree line crackled with blue-green flames.

Somehow, I still had the slingshot in my hand, and I glanced around nervously, looking for the monster. It seemed as if I'd managed to scare it off with that exploding stone, but it would probably be back.

It was then that I looked down and saw it crouching right beside me, its

weaselly face staring up at me in disgust.

"Wrong stone, you idiot."

I leaped away as that strange voice
echoed through my head.

"Hey!" I said, brandishing my empty slingshot. "Don't call me an idiot . . . Wait a second—you can talk?"

The monster rolled its eyes. "Not talk," it said. "Think." It sat back on its haunches like a cat, wings folded neatly and its forked tail wrapped around its feet. I decided to lower my weapon.

"A very wrong stone to be shooting," the monster said. "I did try to warn you."

"By attacking my face?" I replied.

The monster looked even more annoyed.

"Maybe you should say thank you for saving your life?"

I glanced over at the smoldering patch

of ground. The monster had a point.

"Uh, thanks," I said.

"Where is the Guardian?" the monster asked. "The gray-haired one?"

"He's injured," I said. "I'm taking over, just for a while."

I paused, considering the sanity of introducing myself to a flying weasel. Then I did it anyway.

"I'm Leo," I said. "Leo Wilder."

The creature looked up at me, its amber eyes surprised and curious.

"Starla is my name," it said. "And I think you have a lot to learn, Leo Wilder. Like, for example, how to choose the right stone—and also, how to read maps."

"What do you mean?" I asked. "The map led me right to you."

"You are totally sure about that, Leo Wilder?"

I took the map from my pocket. Starla was right; the only light in the clearing was small and amber. This wasn't the monster I was looking for.

I unfolded the map further and there it was: the large purple dot of the Goretusk, glowing brightly and moving fast—

straight toward
the village.

FOUR

I set off into the trees and Starla came after me.

"Are you sure that's the right way, Leo Wilder?" Her voice echoed annoyingly round my head.

"Yes, thank you!" I shouted, pushing my way through the dense undergrowth.

"I think maybe you are lost," Starla called out, perching on a branch just ahead of me.

I stopped, sighing deeply,
then took out the map. Much
as I hated to admit it, the flying
weasel was right.

I could see that the Goretusk was
somewhere near the river, but I didn't
know where *I* was. And every second I
waited, the big purple dot was picking
up speed, zigzagging through the forest
toward the village.

I imagined a huge, shapeless beast
running riot through the village. I pictured
the panic and the hunting parties and
perhaps worst of all, the look on the
Guardian's face when he discovered I'd
let the secret of the monsters get out.

The Goretusk had to be
stopped. And, crazy as it
seemed, it was my job to do it.

So I couldn't refuse Starla's help,
no matter how annoying she was.

"Can you take me to the river?"
I asked. "To the Goretusk?"

She smiled and swished her tail.

"Follow me, Leo Wilder!"

And she flapped off into the trees.

The thick undergrowth made it hard
going, but eventually a path emerged
that led us downhill toward a long strip of
riverside meadow. According to the map,
the monster was here, so when we arrived
at the edge of the trees I stopped and

scanned the meadow carefully. Starla
flew up and down along the tree line,
then swooped down beside me.

"I can smell Goretusk," she said,
wrinkling her nose.

"The monster's not moving," I said. "But
the light on the map's almost half the size
of the meadow. It could be anywhere."

Starla nodded, returning to the
treetops, and I set off along the edge
of the trees, gripping my slingshot
in my hand. I knew we were close,
but the meadow was strangely
quiet. I crouched behind a
mossy hump of rock to think.

Somehow, I needed to draw

the monster out. Then I had to make it turn back upriver and away from the village. I opened up the pouch of stones and looked at the embroidered instructions.

There were twelve different symbols, each with a short, descriptive name. I picked a stone at random and studied its surface in search of the symbol, but as far as I could see it was just a basic gray pebble.

I was about to give up and put it back in the pouch when Starla appeared beside me. She sniffed at the stone.

"Lots of water inside that one," she said.

I frowned at her.

"You can smell what kind of stone it is?"

"Of course," she replied.

I scanned the instructions.

"So, this is a flood-stone?" I asked her.

Starla shrugged. "I suppose you could call it that."

It sounded fine, so I put the stone in my pocket. Starla flapped back into the air, and I shuffled to the edge of the rock to take another look at the meadow.

It was at that moment that the rock

began to move.

A huge tusked head twisted round to face me. Eyes appeared beneath a scaly brow, and a pair of nostrils flared, sending a gust of noxious breath directly into my face.

I scrambled backward, retching at the awful smell, and the mound of rock rose onto four thick legs. This, I realized, was the Armored Goretusk.

I turned and ran, heading for the nearest climbable tree. As I gripped the lower branches, I felt the ground tremble beneath my feet. I glanced back and saw the monster stamping its enormous hooves and scraping dead leaves into the

air with its tusks. It snorted, gouts
of steam blasting from its nostrils.
The look in its eyes was pure anger.
And it was looking at me.

I gripped the branch and began hoisting myself into the tree.

"Climb quicker, Leo Wilder!" Starla called out urgently.

I glanced back from the lowest branch and saw the Goretusk charging right at me.

Springing with all my might, I grabbed on to a higher branch, swinging my legs up just as the Goretusk struck the tree.

The whole world seemed to sway, and the branch vibrated in my hands. Loose bits of foliage rained down on me, and one of my ankles slipped, but I clung on, one leg dangling just a few paces above the monster's tusked head.

The Goretusk struck again, and I felt

my hands begin to lose their grip. Panic surged through me as my fingers slid against the bark.

Being trampled to death by a swamp monster was not how I wanted to end my ninth birthday, so I swung my right arm upward, hooking my elbow round the branch and clasping my other arm as tightly as I could.

My grip was solid now, and in between Goretusk attacks I managed to drag myself up, further and further into the tree until I'd reached a fork about two-thirds of the way up. My arms ached, and when I looked down I felt dizzy and sick from the height.

At least now I was relatively safe, and I took my first real look at my attacker.

The Goretusk was huge, taller than a horse, and about five times heftier. Its back was covered in a kind of bony armor plating, all moldy-looking and sprouting with patches of green vegetation. Its legs were covered in

shaggy black fur, as was its head, which
was home to four long tusks that
curved from the sides of its snouty
face at irregular angles.

It reared up and threw itself against the base of the tree again and again, sending shock waves reverberating up the trunk and through my aching body.

Henrik had been right: this monster certainly was angry.

I wasn't sure how long the tree would last, and I imagined the Village Wall coming under the same assault, splintering as the Goretusk charged through it, turning houses into piles of rubble and trampling anyone unlucky enough to stand in its way.

I had to do something, but all I had was the slingshot and the stones. So far, all I'd managed to do with them was burn down a small section of the forest. I reached into my pocket and pulled out the flood-stone, hoping to do a better job with this one.

But before I could fire, Starla appeared, hovering at my shoulder.

"Not the best stone, Leo Wilder!" she said, sniffing around the pouch at my belt.

I untucked the pouch and opened it up. Seconds later, Starla emerged with a stone between her little pointy teeth.

"This stinky one is good," she said, dropping it into my palm.

I thanked her and loaded the slingshot. I pulled back the stone, peering down through the branches in search of a firing line. The Goretusk thumped itself against the tree, and as the shock wave rippled through me, I thought that maybe, if I timed it right, I stood a chance of hitting my target.

I sat and waited for the monster's next attack. The moment its horned skull appeared between the branches, I let fly with the slingshot.

To my surprise, the stone flew through the branches and struck just as the monster headbutted the tree, exploding over the creature's armored spine in a puff of yellowish gas.

"A not-too-bad shot," commented

Starla. "But maybe try for the head next time?"

Before I could respond, a wave of stink-gas hit me, and the urge to vomit rose up in my throat, stronger than I'd ever felt before. I covered my mouth and nose, fighting to keep my breakfast down. Glancing up, I noticed Starla was hovering clear of the gas cloud, flapping her wings and smiling in such a self-satisfied way that I wanted to leap out of the tree at her.

"See!" she gloated. "Always trust Starla's nose."

FIVE

The stinking cloud of gas began to clear,
and I scanned the forest floor. I couldn't
see the monster, but some distance
away I heard the crash of undergrowth.

The Goretusk was gone.

I climbed down and jogged away
from the sickening stench.

"Fine," I said, as Starla joined me on
the ground. "It worked."

I opened the map, hoping we might have driven the monster away for good, but the purple light was still moving downriver, still on a collision course with the village.

"These stones are useless," I muttered.

"Not useless," said Starla, looking puzzled. "But we have a *very* angry Goretusk here."

"Yeah," I said. "I figured that out already."

I stared at the map, watching the monster's light weave along the course of the river.

"Come on," I said. "Let's go."

◂ ◇ △ ◇ ◂

We arrived at a steep, grassy slope that led down to a narrow section of the river. On the opposite bank, shaking treetops and loud snorting noises gave away the monster's location.

On our side of the river stood a small wooden hut.

"What's that?" I asked Starla, surprised to see a building this far from the village.

"I think that other Guardian made it," she said. "He stays here sometimes, taking fish from the river."

"Right," I said, jogging across the clearing to Henrik's fishing hut.

Behind it, the river ran quick and smooth.

Crashing noises echoed on the opposite bank, but I couldn't see the monster.

"Anything?" I asked Starla, who had perched on the roof.

"Nothing," she said.

I crouched, hidden by the hut, and consulted the map. It showed the Goretusk moving about randomly, and I tried to figure out how long we might have before it reached the village. Then, suddenly, the purple dot wasn't moving quite so randomly anymore.

"Look out!" I screamed to Starla, diving to the side as the hut exploded into splinters and the Goretusk came thundering through.

Fragments of wood rained down around me, but one of the falling bits of wood looked different—it had wings. My heart lurched as Starla crashed to the ground, lying stunned beside the riverbank.

I leaped up and saw the monster thumping its way up the grassy slope toward the trees. But it didn't reach the trees. Instead it stopped, turned around, and charged down the slope at Starla.

With my arms waving above my head, I ran toward Starla.

"Get up!" I shouted. "Fly!"

But she continued to lie still.

The Goretusk was closing in fast, and I was still twenty paces from Starla. I'd never make it in time. So I picked up the first piece of debris I came across and charged at the oncoming monster.

"Hey, stinky breath!" I screamed. "Over here!"

The monster tilted its head my way. A steamy snort escaped its nostrils.

And it changed its course.

I stopped running, feeling a surge of relief that I'd saved Starla from being trampled. The only problem was, now it was coming for me.

I turned and ran toward the river, the earth trembling under my feet. I glanced back and saw several tons of tusked and armored monster bearing down on me so fast I thought my time was up.

Then the river was there, and I was sliding down the bank and pressing myself up against it, waist deep in the cold, fast water. The Goretusk leaped over me, the armor plating and shaggy black fur of its underside blocking out the sun for a terrifying instant.

And it was in that moment that I glimpsed a needle-thin green-and-red spike wedged between two plates of the monster's armor.

That had to be it—the reason for its unstoppable rage.

As it charged through the trees on the opposite bank, I dragged myself, dripping, from the river.

Now, finally, I knew what I had to do.

SIX

I found Starla inspecting her wings
amidst the wreckage of the hut.

"Are you hurt?" I asked.

She looked up and gave me a toothy
grin.

"No," she said. "Which is all thanks to
you, Leo Wilder."

I felt my cheeks flush for a moment.
Then I glanced nervously over what was

left of Henrik's fishing hut. He would not be happy about this.

"Can you fly?" I asked Starla. "We need to get back on the monster's trail."

Starla flapped her wings and rose into the air.

"Ready to go," she said.

We set off downriver, following the purple dot on the map. I jogged as fast as I could in my wet clothes, and Starla flew close above my shoulder. As we weaved through the trees, I told her what I'd seen protruding from the Goretusk's armor.

"Sounds like a Hawkupine quill," said Starla. "Big birds, they are. Very sharp. Very dangerous."

"We have to remove that quill," I said, checking the map as I ran. "It's the only way we're going to stop the monster."

"I think you're right, Leo Wilder," she said. "But getting close won't be totally easy."

She paused, humming thoughtfully for a few seconds.

"You know what?" she said. "I think there is something I need to do."

Then she turned and flapped back upriver at high speed.

"Keep going, Leo Wilder," her voice echoed faintly in my head.

"Hey!" I shouted.

But Starla was gone.

I hurried on through the woodland, feeling very alone. I heard the monster crashing through the trees on the opposite bank, but also another sound: the dull *thock* of timber being chopped. Woodcutters weren't allowed out of sight of the Wall, which meant we were getting dangerously close to the village.

The map showed a sharp bend in the river just ahead. If the monster kept following the river, there was a chance I could cut out the bend and catch up. The trees flashed by, and the sounds of the monster's rampage died away as the river bent away from me.

I wondered where Starla was and what she was doing. But most of all, I wondered what I was going to do when I actually caught up with the monster. There had to be a stone that could help, but they all looked the same. I needed Starla to sniff me out a good one.

Up ahead, I saw that the river was curving back toward me. The map showed the monster darting wildly about on the far side, getting closer. I didn't have long, so I'd just have to pick the stone myself.

I stopped and pulled the instructions from the pouch. Quickly, I scanned down the list of different stones, looking for one that sounded useful.

VANISH-STONE

No.

FIRE-STONE

Definitely no.

SLEEP-STONE

Yes! That was it. If I could put the monster to sleep, then I could remove the Hawkupine quill. Maybe then it would stop trying to destroy everything.

The symbol for the sleep-stone was a set of three different-sized circles, one inside the other like an archery target. I carefully emptied the pouch and hunted through them.

The markings were difficult to see at first, but once I'd found one, it became a little easier each time. Soon I'd picked out all of the sleep-stones—three in total—

and I put these in my pocket and the rest back in the pouch. I rose and hurried on through the forest, the map in one hand and the slingshot in the other.

Soon the river was by my side again, and I peered across to the opposite bank. The undergrowth shook. I heard a thud and saw the top of a tall tree sway, but still I couldn't see the monster. The map showed it nearby, close to the river. I heard another loud crash, and when I looked up there it was, head lowered, horns curving, eyes glaring at me from across the water.

I placed a sleep-stone in the slingshot and took aim.

This was my best chance, perhaps my only one.

The Goretusk snorted, and I released the stone and watched, not daring to breathe, as it flew across the river.

The trajectory looked good, but at the last moment the monster dodged to the side and the stone sank harmlessly into the undergrowth.

My stomach sank as the Goretusk turned and ran. But I ran too, sprinting along the riverbank.

I felt panic grip me. What if that had been my last chance? What if I'd failed? When I reached the village it would be flattened, my mum and sister and

everyone I knew in terrible
danger.

And the secret of the monsters
would be out.

On my first day as a Guardian I'd
ruined everything!

As I ran, I loaded the second sleep-
stone, determined not to let that happen.
I scanned the opposite bank, but the
Goretusk had retreated out of view. I
needed another shot. I needed to get
across the river.

Just then I remembered something
I'd seen on the map. I ran faster, leaping
over tangled roots and crashing through
brambles without a care. And there it

was, at the next gentle bend in the river:
a grassy clearing and a wooden bridge.

I ran onto the bridge and paused
midway. To my right, downriver,
I could see the Village Wall rising above
the trees. The sounds of village life
drifted faintly on the breeze.
I stared ahead into the forest. No

sign of the monster.

But the map showed it was there,
moving toward the village.

I took a deep breath, ready for the
final chase.

"Wait!" a voice echoed in my head.
"Leo Wilder!"

I turned and saw Starla land in the small clearing behind me. She dropped a huge pile of soggy green vegetation from her mouth, then spat and shook her head in disgust.

"Ugh," she said. "This bog-weed is totally the worst."

"What are you doing?" I asked, wrinkling my nose at the revolting, swampy smell. "The monster's almost at the village. I have to find it!"

"It will come to you, Leo Wilder. Just wait and see."

"What are you talking about? We don't have time for this."

I stood on the bridge, trying to decide if I believed her, the precious seconds ticking away. Then I noticed Starla was staring past me, with a look of deep concern in her little amber eyes.

"I think maybe you should get off the bridge now," she said.

I heard a loud snort behind me.

Glancing down at the map, I saw the river and the bridge and a big purple light right on top of it.

I ran toward Starla and heard the thump of hooves behind me. The slingshot was already in my hands, and as I reached the end of the bridge, I turned and fired the stone.

It missed by a finger's width and the Goretusk charged on, its hooves so loud I thought the bridge might collapse beneath them.

Backing up, I fumbled the final sleep-stone from my pocket. My boots squelched through the pile of bog-weed as the monster came thundering off the end of the bridge. Its eyes locked furiously with mine, and I knew that if I missed, I would be trampled into the ground.

I raised the slingshot, took aim, and fired the stone.

It struck the monster directly on the snout, exploding into a dense bubble of dark-blue liquid that covered the creature's face. For a terrifying moment, the monster ran on, but now its eyes were closed, and its mouth hung open.

Its legs gave way, and its huge body crashed to the ground, skidding through the grass until it ground to a halt, snoring, right at my feet.

SEVEN

The Goretusk had collapsed onto its side and it took all of our combined strength to tilt its body so that I could pull the Hawkupine quill free. I leaped away, expecting the pain to wake the monster into another fit of rage. But the sleep-stone was strong, and the monster barely stirred.

By the time it woke, I was hiding

in a nearby tree with the colorful quill in my knapsack and Starla perching beside me. I had the slingshot out, with another stink-stone loaded in case the monster woke up angry.

Luckily for everyone, the Goretusk woke groggy and confused, shuffling around the clearing and occasionally licking at the wound on its shoulder. Pretty soon it was munching contentedly at the bog-weed, its tail flicking gently from side to side.

"I wish you'd told me where you were going," I said to Starla. "I thought you'd left me."

"Leave you?" She seemed shocked.

"You saved me, Leo Wilder, so now we work together, yes?"

"Uh . . . Yes," I said. "Thanks."

I watched the Goretusk quietly work through the pile of bog-weed.

"Do you think it's safe to climb down?" I asked Starla.

"Let me go first," she said, flapping cautiously toward the monster.

The creature raised its head when Starla approached, but all it did was let out a quick snort before going back to the bog-weed. It really did love that stuff.

Starla nodded to me, and I began climbing down from the tree.

Without the quill in its shoulder,

the Goretusk was calm, even friendly. I held a handful of the bog-weed in front of its four-horned snout, and it lurched toward me, making my heart leap. But it slurped the food in carefully, leaving my hand wet, but thankfully still attached to my arm.

I scooped up the rest of the bog-weed and led the creature over the bridge, making sure we were well away from the village and the woodcutters before I dropped the food and let the monster eat.

"Can you find some more?" I asked Starla.

"Of course," she said, eagerly flapping away.

While she was gone, I examined the map, tracing the river northeast toward its source in the mountains. A few miles upriver, I found the cluster of purple lights Henrik had pointed out that morning. They were mostly stationary, gathered around an area of marshland called the Festian Swamps.

"Don't worry," I told the Goretusk as it happily chewed on its meal. "We'll get you home."

I led the monster slowly upriver while Starla flew back and forth, tearing up bog-weed from the riverbanks wherever she could find it. The sun reached its noonday peak, then began to descend. It was almost touching the distant western mountaintops by the time we reached our destination.

The trees thinned out, and the river split into a series of shallow channels that spread across a flat expanse of marshland. Tufts of grass grew everywhere, and a few low, gnarled trees dangled their branches into the water. The early evening sunlight slanted down on the marsh, picking out a series of rocky islands, some no larger than stepping stones, others easily big enough to build a house on. Behind it all were the first steep, forested foothills, rising toward the looming mountain peaks.

As soon as we neared the marsh's edge, the Goretusk lumbered forward and stuck its face into the water, emerging with a huge mouthful of bog-weed.

I examined the map, puzzled.

"There should be loads more Goretusks around here," I said to Starla.

Starla nudged me with her wing.

"Leo Wilder," she said. "Look."

The islands had begun to move.

Water poured from their mossy, armored backs as they rose from the water. Curved horns glistened in the sun, and a deep, mournful song echoed round the marsh.

Our Goretusk returned the call and slowly waded into the water.

"It's just a child," I said, staring in wonder as the monster that had seemed so huge and dangerous was surrounded by creatures four or five times larger. Waves spread across the marsh as they moved, and the air vibrated with their booming welcome calls.

◂ ◊ △ ◊ ▸

We headed back downriver, Starla weaving through the branches above me. I wanted to rush home and tell Mum and Lulu and Jacob everything that had happened. But I couldn't tell anybody. I had to keep the monsters a secret.

The true weight of my Assignment settled on my heart.

But then, I remembered, I wasn't alone.

"Have you seen the Goretusks' home before?" I asked Starla.

"Not really, Leo Wilder," she said. "The smell is bad, so I always fly past quickly.

I didn't know marsh monsters could be
so grand like that. They were pleased to
see their young one."

"Yes," I said. "They were."

I looked up at Starla, watching her

stubby legs flail as she dipped and turned, her wings flapping and gliding and her forked tail flowing behind. She was such a strange creature, but I supposed humans would probably seem strange if you'd never seen one before.

"Do you have a herd?" I asked her. "A family of other . . .?"

I trailed off, realizing I didn't know what kind of monster she was.

"Leatherwings," she said.

She went quiet for a moment, and I remembered that her dot on the map was amber colored. She wasn't one of the four types of monster Henrik had mentioned.

"My family is far away," Starla said. "Far beyond the mountains. That's where I'm from. That's where my herd was living."

I wanted to ask how she'd come to the forest and why she was all alone, but she flapped her leathery wings and pushed on ahead of me.

"Hurry up with your legs, Leo Wilder," she said. "The sun is almost gone."

EIGHT

I peered through the trees at the Guardian's cabin, a thin plume of wood smoke rising from its roof.

"Time for me to go," said Starla.

"Right," I said, feeling slightly awkward. "Thanks for all your help."

Starla grinned.

"See you again, Leo Wilder!"

Then she flapped away from me,

disappearing

into the forest.

The cabin door creaked.

"So you're still alive," Henrik called, peering out at me from a brightly lit doorway. "I suppose you'd better come in."

Inside, Henrik handed me a clay bowl of something warm and dark and told me to sit.

"My own recipe," the Guardian said. "Ginger and yarlroot tea. It'll keep you going after a long day fighting monsters."

I perched on a large storage chest and sipped the tea cautiously. It was hot but not scalding, with a strong ginger taste, but also a hint of wood smoke and honey. I took another sip before carefully placing the steaming bowl of tea on the floor.

"I found this wedged into the Goretusk's armor," I said, retrieving the quill from my knapsack and holding it out for Henrik.

"Hmm, yes," he said, examining the red-and-green spike with a strange expression on his face.

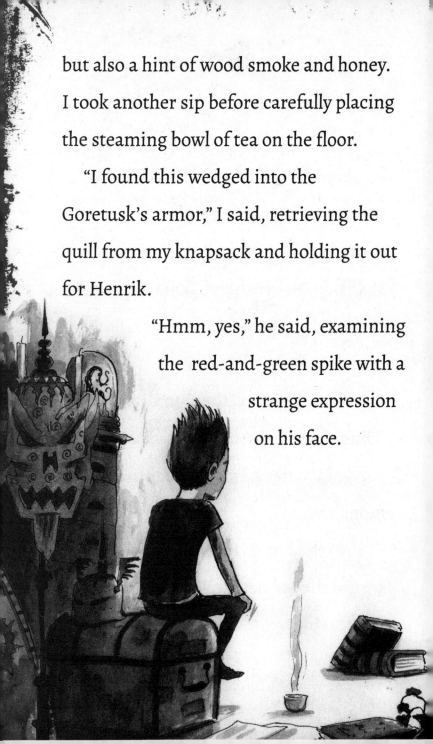

"Must have been attacked by a Hawkupine."

He dropped the quill into a large clay pot that bristled with an alarming assortment of objects: sharpened wooden sticks, heavy-looking spears, and jagged harpoons. There were also

what looked like several other quills, similar to the one I'd pulled from the Goretusk.

I gave Henrik a quizzical look.

"Don't Hawkupines hunt in the mountains?" I asked him.

The Guardian narrowed his eyes.

"Who told you that?" he replied. "The Leatherwing, I suppose?"

I nodded.

"Well," he said. "She's half right. But Hawkupines have been known to stray into the forest, and they're strong enough to carry off a baby Goretusk if they can't find anything else to eat."

He raised his eyebrows and drank

a sip of tea, as if to signal that the discussion was over. But I wasn't sure I believed him. I took another long look at the clay pot, wondering if he did indeed have a collection of Hawkupine quills in there.

"Better drink your tea, boy. Before it gets cold."

He leaned back in his chair, obscuring my view of the quills, and we sipped our tea in silence.

Eventually Henrik slurped up the last of his drink and set his bowl down on the desk with a thud. I looked up and found him smiling at me.

"You did all right today, boy," he said.

I felt a rush of pride, taking another sip of tea to hide my smile.

"You understand what it means to be a Guardian now?" he asked me. "What it means to the forest, to the people of the village?"

"I do," I replied.

Henrik nodded, leaning back in his chair, weighing me up like he had when we'd first met.

"You're a good lad," he said. "Now finish up your drink. You don't want to be walking these woods in the dark."

◂ ◇ △ ◇ ▸

I hurried through the tangle of thorns outside the cabin. It was almost night, and the trees cast a dense web of shadows around me. When I reached the tall, pointed stone I felt a rush of relief; here was the path that would take me home.

I'd left the Map of Monsters with the Guardian, along with the stones and the slingshot. Although I was glad to leave the cabin behind, I already missed the map, and I missed Starla too. Just a little.

I arrived at the Village Wall and found Gilda sitting on a moldy tree stump. When she saw me, she leaped to her feet, smiling and clapping me on the shoulder as if I'd risen from the dead.

"I guess *you* didn't expect me to survive either?" I said.

"Ridiculous! I knew you'd be fine," she replied, though her awkward smile suggested otherwise. "And the

monster . . ." she whispered. "It's . . .?"

"Yes!" I said, sighing. "It's back home with its family."

"Oh, good," said Gilda. "That *is* good news."

"Hopefully its shoulder will heal properly," I added. "That quill left a nasty wound."

"Yes, of course," she said. "Of course."

She led me to the secret door in the Village Wall, but she turned to me before opening it.

"Leo," she said. "You did well today. You've proven yourself worthy of this Assignment. But now you have a choice; you must decide if you want to become a Guardian. You have to be sure, so if you'd rather not do it, we can move you to the Records Office. That's where you always wanted to go, isn't it?"

"Uh, yes," I said, taken off guard. "I don't know if . . ."

"It's all right," Gilda cut in. "You don't have to decide right now. Take the night to think about it."

She unlocked the secret door and swung it open for me.

"Just remember," she whispered as we stepped inside. "If you accept this Assignment, you can never tell anyone what you really do. Not family. Not friends. No one."

I nodded, letting it sink in slowly as
we crept past the turnip man, who was
still slumped and snoring in his chair.
He hadn't moved an inch since the
morning.

We made our way through the village,
and Gilda explained how things would
work. If I wanted to, I could start at the
Records Office in the morning, telling
anyone who asked that I'd been helping
her with some secret council business
for the day.

Or I could accept the Guardian
Assignment.

"If you choose to become a Guardian,
you'll need a cover story," Gilda said.

"We'll go with 'Forest Maintenance.' That way, if anyone sees you outside the Wall, you've got a perfectly good explanation."

It made sense, but the thought of lying to my family made me feel strange. And how was I supposed to choose? I thought about the forest and the map, about Starla, and the Goretusks at home in the swamp. Then I thought about Henrik. If I accepted the Assignment, would I end up alone in the forest like him?

We arrived at the street where I lived, and all the familiar sights and sounds crashed in on me. Suddenly, nothing I'd seen or done in the forest seemed real.

Gilda patted me on the back.

"Now go in and enjoy the rest of your birthday," she said.

◂ ◊ △ ◊ ▸

"Leo!" Mum said as I stepped inside.

She rushed over and gave me a hug. When she let go, I saw that Jacob and Lulu were sitting at the table, which had been laid with plates of flatbreads, cheese, and fruit. In the middle

was a big honey cake—my absolute
favorite—and I suddenly felt incredibly
hungry.

"Sit down," Mum said. "Go on!"

I slid onto my chair and smiled at
Jacob, who looked even
more eager than me
to start on the honey
cake.

"Jacob was just telling me about his day in the Records Office," Lulu said.

I could tell she was trying not to smirk. Jacob had a habit of exaggerating, so Lulu never believed a word he said.

"It was great," Jacob said. "Master Aldred fell asleep as soon as he'd eaten his breakfast, so I did whatever I wanted all day. I wish you'd been there. It was great."

I wanted to tell him I'd be there in the Records Office tomorrow. I knew it would be great to spend my Assignment with Jacob. We'd have so much fun, and the work would be easy.

But I held back.

This decision wasn't just about me; it was about the village and the creatures of the forest, too. And when I thought about Master Aldred and the Records Office, it seemed different now. I'd seen a whole other world outside the village. I'd saved a monster and made friends with another. Could I really just forget all of that and go back to messing about with Jacob in the Records Office?

I noticed that Lulu and Jacob were both watching me curiously.

"Well," Lulu said. "Whatever top secret work Leo's been doing, it's definitely tired him out."

Jacob laughed, then he leaned

forward on his elbows, his eyes intense. "Can you tell us?" he whispered. "What's the big secret?"

I nodded. "I was helping Gilda with some village council stuff—just for today."

"Is that it?" Jacob asked, clearly disappointed. "So what's your proper Assignment?"

And suddenly I knew. I wanted to hold the Map of Monsters again, to study those strange moving lights. I wanted to see Starla again, too, and above all, I wanted to help keep the village and the monsters safe.

A smile crept across my face as the

weight of the decision lifted.

"Forest maintenance," I said, shrugging as casually as I could. "Just forest maintenance."

THE ARMORED GORETUSK

STRENGTH	10
SIZE	9
SPEED	7
INTELLIGENCE	4
WEAPONRY	8

MONSTER TYPE
Swamp Monster

HABITAT
Festian Swamps

FOOD
Bog-weed, low shrubs, and leaf mulch

ATTACK STYLE

The Armored Goretusk is herbivorous, but will charge when provoked, using its considerable weight and its four long, curved tusks to destroy or impale anything in its path.

DESCRIPTION

A large, four-legged monster with an armor-plated back and four irregular tusks. Young Goretusks can measure up to six paces in length and three in height. Adult Goretusks can be up to twenty-five paces long. The armor plating on a Goretusk's back provides protection from predators and is often covered with moss and other vegetation. Goretusks rarely leave their swamp habitat, preferring to wallow in the water in herds, feasting on the foul-smelling bog-weed that lies just below the surface.

THE LEATHER-WING

STRENGTH	2
SIZE	2
SPEED	9
INTELLIGENCE	10
WEAPONRY	4

MONSTER TYPE
Desert Monster

HABITAT
Clay Desert

FOOD
Insects and fruit

ATTACK STYLE

Though small, Leatherwings can be ferocious, and will use their sharp teeth and claws to fend off predators. Their agility in the air makes them very successful insect hunters.

DESCRIPTION

The Leatherwing is a small, furry, four-legged creature that flies using its oversize, featherless wings. Leatherwings live together in large families, or "clan groups," traveling across the vast Clay Desert in search of seasonal feeding grounds. Leatherwing clan groups often build temporary burrows in the walls of ravines, their sand-colored fur providing highly efficient camouflage.

THE STONES

FIRE-STONE

STINK-STONE

VANISH-STONE

SLEEP-STONE

FLOOD-STONE

CHOOSE YOUR STONES WISELY . . .

READ ON FOR A
SNEAK PEEK AT LEO'S
NEXT ADVENTURE . . .

LEO'S MAP OF MONSTERS

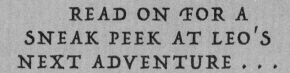

THE SPITFANG LIZARD

A cold wind raced through the forest, shaking the trees and pelting me with dead autumn leaves. I crept through the undergrowth with my slingshot loaded and ready, scanning the treetops and listening hard for any sign of movement.

Somewhere close by there was a Treeshark, a monster so rare and deadly that even Henrik had seemed afraid when he'd spoken its name. Apparently, Treesharks hibernated for ten or twelve years at a time, high up near the mountains, but when they woke they liked nothing better than to set out on a weeklong feeding frenzy down in the forest.

A crashing noise behind me made me turn, my slingshot raised and my heart pounding. I stared into the canopy, straining to spot the hulking, irregular shadow Henrik had warned me about.

But there was no shadow, just a large branch clattering its way toward the forest floor, torn from its trunk by the wind.

I continued on my way, creepin

deeper and deeper into the forest.

A few minutes later, at the base of a shallow slope, I paused.

There was something up ahead.

I peered through the trembling branches, up the slope and into the canopy of one of the taller yew trees. There was a shadow: large, many-limbed, and deathly still between the boughs of the tree.

I swallowed hard and raised my slingshot.

KRIS HUMPHREY

Kris has done his fair share of interesting jobs (cinema projectionist, blood factory technician, bookseller, teacher). But he's always been writing—or at least thinking about writing.

In 2012 Kris graduated with distinction from the MA in Writing for Young People at Bath Spa University, winning the award for Most Promising Writer. He is the author of two series of books for young readers: *Guardians of the Wild* and now, *Leo's Map of Monsters*.

ABOUT THE ILLUSTRATOR
PETE WILLIAMSON

Pete is a London-based writer, illustrator, and animation designer, who has illustrated over 65 books including *Stitch Head* and *Skeleton Keys: The Unimaginary Friend.*

Read all of Leo's incredible adventures!